# Michael Jordan

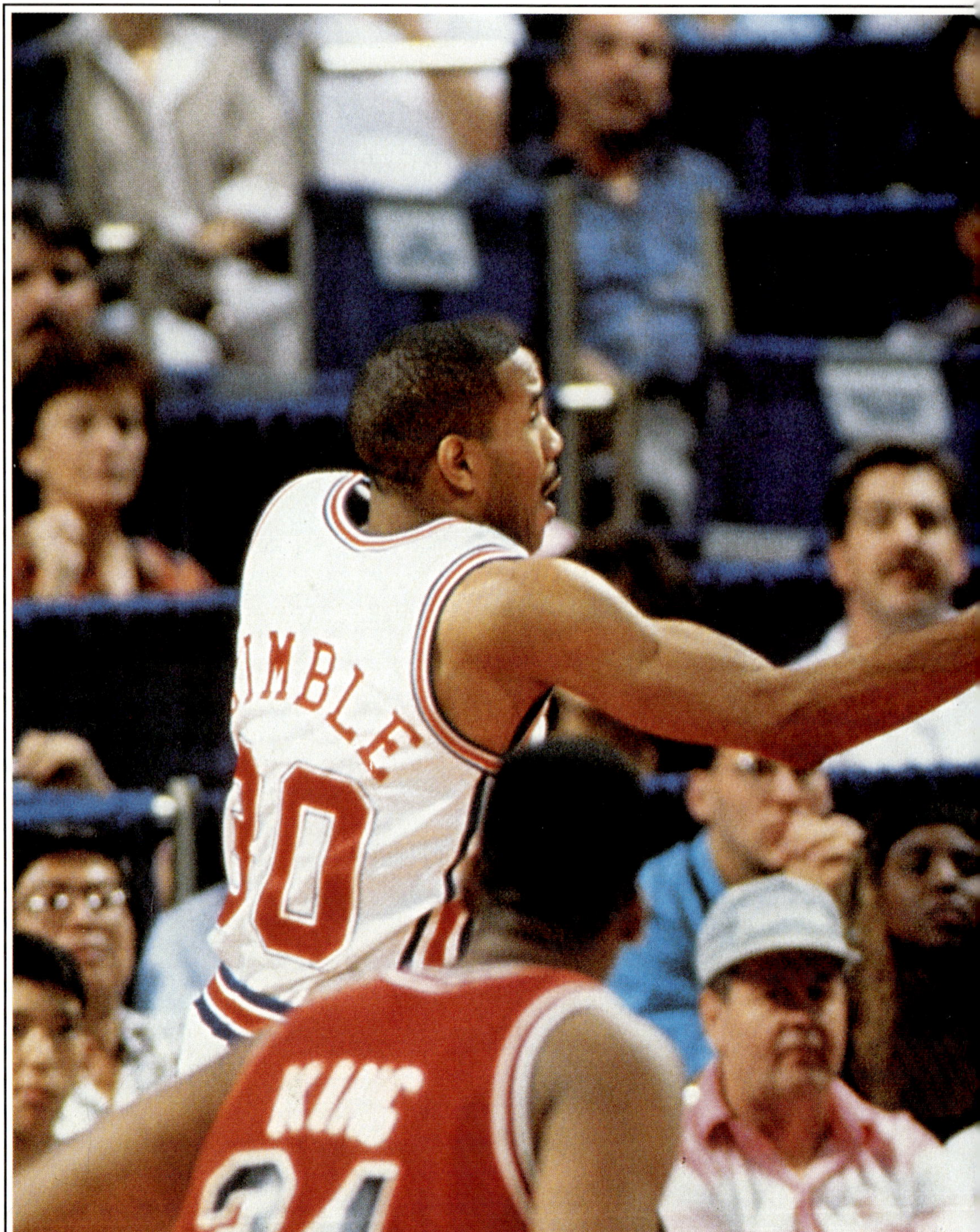
KING
34

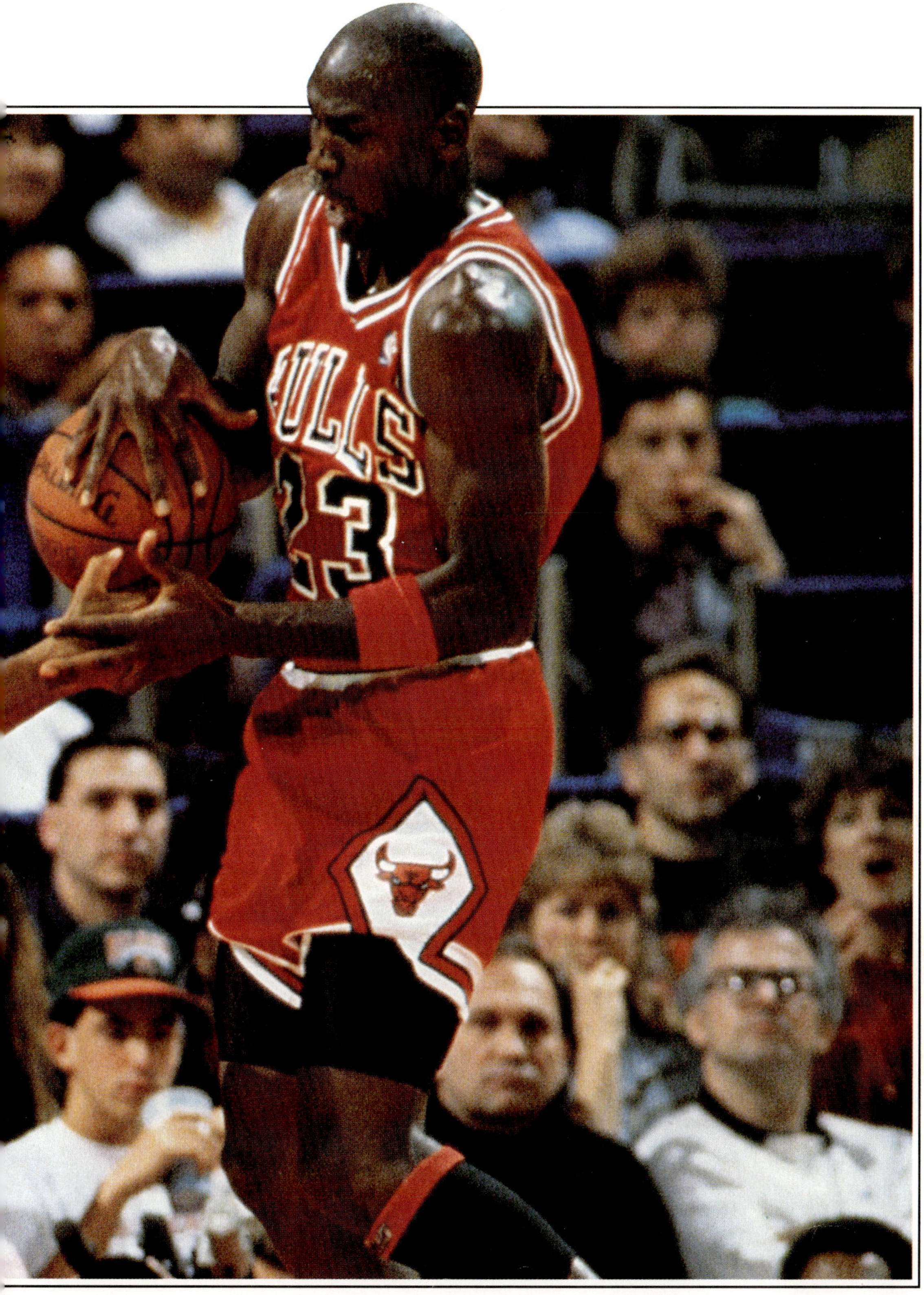

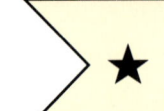

PHOTO CREDITS
The National Basketball Association
Nathaniel Butler: cover, pg. 9, 10, 13, 17, 18, 25, 26
Andrew Bernstein: pg. 2 & 3 and pg. 21
Allsport: pg. 6, 14, 22, 29 and 30

Text copyright © 1991 by The Child's World, Inc.
All rights reserved. No part of this book may be
reproduced or utilized in any form or by any means
without written permission from the Publisher.
Printed in the United States of America.

Distributed to Schools and Libraries
in the United States by
ENCYCLOPAEDIA BRITANNICA EDUCATIONAL CORP.
310 S. Michigan Avenue
Chicago, Illinois 60604

Library of Congress Cataloging-in-Publication Data
Rothaus, James.
 Michael Jordan / Jim Rothaus.
  p. cm.
 Summary: A brief career biography of the talented,
 seemingly unstoppable, Chicago Bull.
  ISBN 0-89565-733-3
 1. Jordan, Michael, 1963-  —Juvenile literature.
 2. Basketball players—United States—Biography—Juvenile literature.
 [1. Jordan, Michael, 1963-  2. Basketball players.
 3. Afro-Americans—Biography.] I. Title.
 GV884.J67R68  1991           91-18585
 796.323′092—dc20              CIP
    [B]                        AC

# Michael Jordan

by James R. Rothaus

Michael at 1991 NBA All-Star Game.

## Big Shot Is Needed

Time was running out on the University of North Carolina in the 1982 NCAA national championship game. The Tar Heels were behind Georgetown 62-61 with less than thirty seconds to play. North Carolina point guard Jimmy Black got a pass from Matt Doherty. He looked inside for the Heels' veteran stars, James Worthy and Sam Perkins. Neither was open. Black then whipped the ball across the court to Michael Jordan, North Carolina's outstanding freshman.

# A Legend Is Born

With less than twenty seconds to go, Jordan shot a seventeen-foot jumper that swished through the basket. North Carolina's youngest starter had made the biggest shot of the season. The Tar Heels won 63-62, and the legend of Michael Jordan was born. Jordan stayed at North Carolina two more years. In fact, he was named College Player of the Year both of those seasons. With nothing left to prove at the college level, Jordan left school after his junior year. He entered the National Basketball Association draft.

**Jordan directs the offense.**

**Michael is an offensive machine.**

## Rookie of the Year

The Chicago Bulls had the third pick in the 1984 draft. They used it to take the six-foot-six Jordan. Jordan might have been the third pick in the draft, but he soon proved he was the number one rookie in the NBA. Jordan averaged more than twenty-three points a game. He was named NBA Rookie of the Year for the 1984-85 season. But the rookie wasn't finished. In the first round of the playoffs, the Bulls played defending NBA champion Boston.

## NBA Playoff Scoring Record

The experts gave Chicago no chance to upset the powerful Celtics in the best-of-five series. Michael Jordan, though, nearly led the young Bulls to a big upset. He scored forty-nine points in the first game of the series. But Chicago couldn't defeat Larry Bird and the Celtics. In the second game, Jordan put on the best performance in the history of the NBA playoffs. He scored sixty-three points, an all-time league playoff record. Despite his efforts, Chicago lost again.

**Michael nearly leads Bulls to an upset.**

**Jordan nicknamed Superman.**

## 'No One Can Guard Him'

After the game sportswriters crowded around the locker of Boston guard Dennis Johnson, who had tried to stop Jordan. Johnson had been named to the NBA All-Defensive Team eight times. He was a player who had shut down most of the top guards in the league over the years. What about Michael Jordan?, they asked Johnson. "As you can see," a tired Johnson said, "no one can guard him." Michael Jordan was no longer a superstar. He was Superman.

## Wings on His Feet

"It must be like most of the rest of us [NBA players] playing with grade-school kids," said Chicago point guard John Paxson of Jordan. "That's how good he is." Jordan was so good, he sometimes even surprised himself. "I wish I could show you a film of a dunk I had in Milwaukee," Jordan told a magazine writer. "It's in slow motion. It looks like I'm taking off, like somebody put wings on me. I get chills when I see it."

*A slam dunk.*

**Jordan doesn't jump. He flies.**

## An Incredible Leaper

Other NBA players get chills when they think about trying to guard Jordan. He's fast. He's amazingly quick. And probably no basketball player has ever been able to jump like Jordan can. Some opponents believe that Jordan doesn't jump. He flies. "He has different skills than the rest of us," said Cleveland guard Craig Ehlo. Jordan, though, wasn't always a star basketball player.

## First Love Was Baseball

Growing up in Wilmington, North Carolina, Jordan's first love was baseball, not basketball. In fact, he didn't play much basketball until his junior year in high school. Jordan grew four inches between his sophomore and junior years. He then decided his future was on the basketball court, not the baseball diamond. Michael and older brother Larry made Laney High School an excellent basketball team. Larry was almost a foot shorter than Michael. But he actually was the better player at first.

**Michael grew up in North Carolina.**

**Mr. Unstoppable.**

## Tongue Hangs Out

Michael had a strange habit when he played. His tongue would hang out while he moved up and down the court. "My father used to have his tongue out when he'd be working, doing mechanical stuff," Jordan remembered. "I just picked it up from him." By the time he graduated from high school, the tongue-wagging Jordan was one of the best college prospects in the country. Then it came time to pick a college. Jordan's mother, Delores, wanted him to go to North Carolina.

## Olympic Stardom After College

At first Michael didn't really like North Carolina, but his mother talked him into going. Jordan's parents, Delores and James, attended every college game their son played, at home and away. After ending his college career, Jordan starred on the gold medal-winning 1984 United States Olympic Team. "Playing with him was like going to the circus," said fellow Olympic Team member Waymon Tisdale. "You'd come to practice and never know what he'd pull off."

*A member of the 1984 Olympic Team.*

**Jordan takes the Bulls to the top.**

## Making the Bulls into a Contender

Once Jordan got to the pros, some experts wondered how well he would do. Chicago had been a bad team in the years before Jordan joined the club. And Michael Jordan wasn't used to playing on bad teams. His high school and college teams were great clubs. Could Jordan lift the Bulls to a championship level? He did, slowly but surely. The Bulls improved a little every year. Jordan, meanwhile, became the best scorer in the league.

## NBA Scoring Champ, 1987-1990

In his third pro season, Jordan averaged an amazing 37.1 points a game in 1987. Only Wilt Chamberlain had ever scored more points in a season. Jordan also won the NBA scoring titles in 1988, 1989, and 1990. He averaged more than thirty points a game in each of those seasons. He also became only the second player to win four straight league scoring titles. Behind Jordan's play, Chicago made it all the way to the Eastern Conference finals in both 1989 and 1990. Each time the Bulls were defeated by the Detroit Pistons. Detroit went on to win the NBA championship both times.

**Michael has his eyes set on an NBA championship.**

**Just stay close.**

## Special Defense for Jordan

**D**etroit, in fact, was so afraid of Jordan that the Pistons created a special defense to stop him. Despite this defense, the Bulls are confident they can beat any team in the NBA. That's because Jordan is just so special. "What I'm trying to convince the guys of is to just stay close for three quarters," said former Chicago coach Doug Collins. "Then we've got something spectacular to use." That spectacular item is Michael Jordan, one of the most talented, exciting players in the history of the NBA.